Meet the Author
www.darylcobb.com

Daryl Cobb lives in New Jersey with his wife and two children. Daryl's writing began in college as a Theatre Arts major at Virginia Commonwealth University. He found a freshman writing class inspiring and, combined with his love for music and the guitar, he discovered a passion for songwriting. This talent would motivate him for years to come and the rhythm he created with his music also found its way into the bedtime stories he later created for his children. The story "Boy on the Hill," about a boy who turns the clouds into animals, was his first bedtime story/song and was inspired by his son and an infatuation with the shapes of clouds. Through the years his son and daughter have inspired so much of his work, including "Daniel Dinosaur" and "Daddy Did I Ever Say? I Love You, Love You, Every Day."

Daryl spends a lot of his time these days visiting schools promoting literacy with his interactive educational assemblies "Teaching Through Creative Arts: A Writer's Journey." These performance programs teach children about the writing and creative process and allow Daryl to do what he feels is most important -- inspire children to read and write. He also performs at benefits and libraries with his "Music & Storytime" shows.

Meet the Illustrator
www.margotmiller.com

Other books by Daryl K. Cobb:

"Do Pirates Go To School?"

"Pirates: Legend of the Snarlyfeet

"Bill the Bat Baby Sits Bella"

"Bill the Bat Finds His Way Home"

"Bill the Bat Loves Halloween"

"Barnyard Buddies: Perry Parrot Finds a Purpose"

"Daddy Did I Ever Say? I Love You,
   Love You, Every Day"

"Daniel Dinosaur"

"Boy on the Hill"

"Count With Daniel Dinosaur"

Find all of Daryl's books at www.darylcobb.com

Printed in the USA
Published by 10 To 2 Children's Books

Henry Hare's

Written by
Daryl K. Cobb

Illustrated by
Margot Miller

Floppy Socks

10 To 2 Children's Books / Clinton

ISBN 978-0615796109

Written by Daryl K. Cobb
Illustrated by Margot Miller

10 To 2 Children's Books

Time to Read

™

For Cameron and Kayley
and all those kids who love to hop.
Daryl K. Cobb

To Rachel, my muse-a-gogo.
Margot Miller

To: Zoe
Have Fun reading.
Daryl K Cobb

Henry Hare loved to hop.

He'd hop and hop, he could not stop.

But every time he'd turn around

he'd find his socks had fallen down.

He'd pull them up

as *high* as *they'd* **go.**

He'd take three hops and they'd fall low.

He'd pull them UP and they'd fall down.

Up and down and up and down.

"I just can't hop with floppy socks!"

said Henry Hare to Linda Sue.

"Floppy Socks?"
said Linda Sue.
"Did you try tape,
or maybe glue?"

"Linda, Linda, Linda Sue. With all this hair glue won't do."

"Bubble gum?"

"Bubble gum?

Now that's just dumb.
I can't use tape.
I can't use glue.

GLUE

And bubble gum? That just won't do."

"You could tie them up with a string, or a rubber band might be the thing."

"A rubber band,"
said Henry Hare,
"might be the thing
that keeps them there."

Peter, Paul and Peggy Pup
said, "Yes,
that just might keep them up.

But remember this,
we say to you,
your legs will turn
a purple-blue.

Your feet will then
just fall asleep.
You'll hop no more
with sleepy feet."

"Sleepy feet?" said Linda Sue.

"What is Henry supposed to do?

He can't use tape.

He can't use glue.

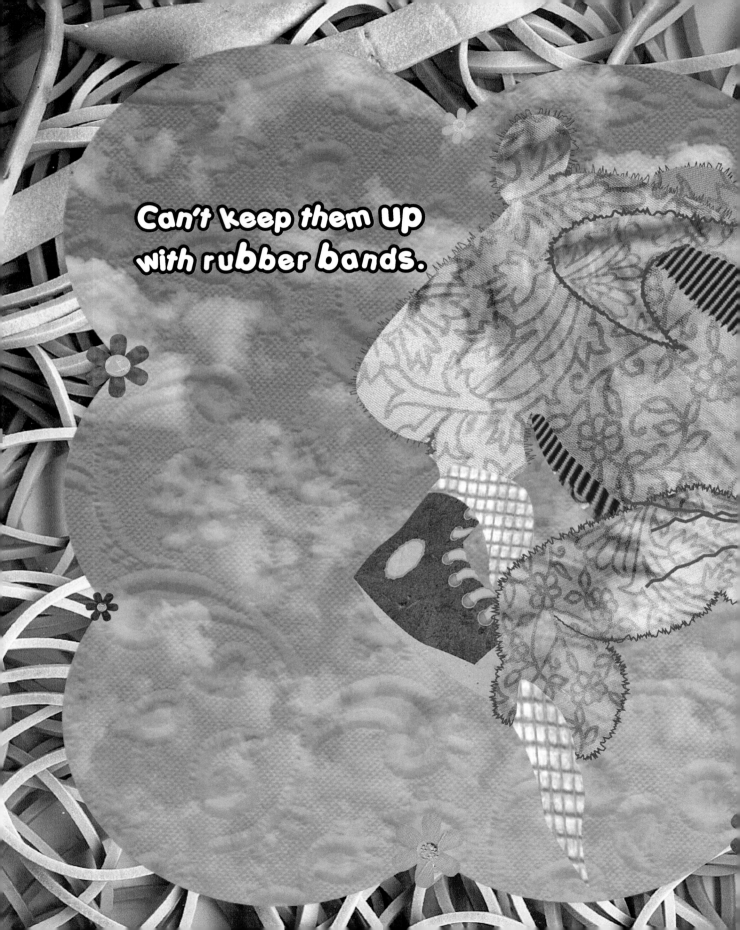

Can't keep them up with rubber bands.

Can't hop and hold them with his **hands.**"

A voice **echoed** from a *tree,*
"Henry, Henry,
look at me."

They all looked up
and saw him there.

It was Al the owl
with his brilliant stare.

"I have just one thing
I need to say,
then it's back to sleep,
if I may:

Suspenders!~

Suspenders!"

Pirates: The Ring of Hope

"Cobb's 14th book comes complete with pirates, mysterious messages and a magic ring . . .. The characters are rich and beautifully rendered, and the story is sprinkled with humor . . .. Much of the dialogue is delightfully silly.

. . . [A] spirited swashbuckling tale of mystery and magic."
-- Kirkus Reviews

Mr. Moon

"A pleasing children's narrative with a relevant message. ... Cobb's text ... has a simple charm likely to please young readers [and]. . . Jaeger's illustrations give the night a soft, beautiful glow, complementing Cobb's text . . .. Her personifications of Mr. Moon and Mr. Sun are utterly delightful."
-- Kirkus Reviews

Daddy Did I Ever Say? I Love You, Love You, Every Day

"A cute, curly-haired, kindergarten-aged girl opens the story by asking her father if she's ever told him how much she loves him . . . the sentiment is sweet and Van Wagoner's illustrations are eye catching. . .. The verse Cobb has penned is appealing and . . . [t]he idea behind the story of the little girl and her doting father is charming[.] " -- Kirkus Reviews

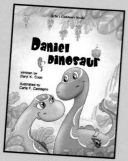

Daniel Dinosaur

"A sweet story told in simple rhymes that young children will likely enjoy. Cobb and Castangno's cute, colorful picture book illustrates the bond between a brother and sister." -- Kirkus Reviews

Bill the Bat Baby Sits Bella

"A sweet book celebrating brother-sister bonds."
-- Kirkus Reviews

Bill the Bat Loves Halloween

"A fast- moving, fun rhyming picture book . . .."
-- Kirkus Reviews

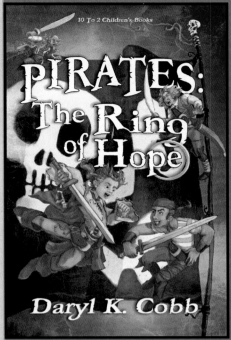

Pirates: The Ring of Hope
Children's Novel/Chapter Book
for advanced young readers
or ages 10-14 and up

Books & Music
by Daryl K. Cobb

Author Visits and School Program
information at www.darylcobb.com

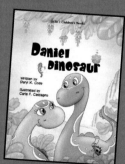

29226461R00022

Made in the USA
Middletown, DE
11 February 2016